CLASS ELECTION

THE SECRETS TO

RU...

SCH...

AMULET BOOKS
NEW YORK

CLASS

ELECTION

NEIL SWAAB

Library of Congress Cataloging-in-Publication Data

Names: Swaab, Neil, author, illustrator.

Title: Class election / Neil Swaab.

Description: New York : Amulet Books, 2016. | Series: The secrets to ruling school ; 2 |
Summary: Self-proclaimed middle school expert and campaign manager Max Corrigan
offers advice and practical tips on how to run for class president and win votes,
including the essential skills needed to make a viral video, trade your lunch in the
school cafeteria, and put a positive spin on any situation.

Identifiers: LCCN 2016007665 (print) | LCCN 2016023010 (ebook)
ISBN 9781419721267 (hardback) | ISBN 9781613121207 (ebook)

Subjects: | CYAC: Middle schools—Fiction. | Schools—Fiction. |Elections—Fiction. |
Interpersonal relations—Fiction. | Humorous stories. | BISAC: JUVENILE FICTION /
School & Education. | JUVENILE FICTION / Humorous Stories. | JUVENILE FICTION /
Comics & Graphic Novels / General.

Classification: LCC PZ7.1.S92 Cl 2016 (print) | LCC PZ7.1.S92 (ebook) | DDC
[Fic]—dc23

LC record available at https://lccn.loc.gov/2016007665

ABRAMS The Art of Books
115 West 18th Street, New York, NY 10011
abramsbooks.com

To Sally

MONDAY

CHAPTER ONE

Move Along

Don't you know that tardiness is the leading cause of moral decay in this school? It's a gateway offense—one morning you're late to social studies, and the next you're doing a five-year stretch in juvie with your new pals Stabby Face and Toe Jam and the outside world is a distant memory.

So go on and hurry up. Unless you want to miss class, wreck your life, and become a degenerate criminal with no future, independence, or—

What? You didn't think I turned into some kind of narc since the last time you saw me, did you? No way—this hall monitor shtick's just another one of my patented ploys! Thanks to this homemade sash, I can wander around the school anywhere, anytime, no questions asked. Total freedom, baby!

Man, middle school sure is a piece of cake. And I hope you agree now that you're settled in.

Sorry I've been MIA the past few weeks—there have been a busload of changes here at William H. Taft to keep my eye on. My business is booming, Kevin Carl's out of the picture, and my dad, Principal Sitz, is at some kind of educational summit for the month, so now Vice Principal Hartley's in charge. And she's *definitely* not my father.

Of course, not every transformation has been as positive. Thanks to budget cuts, the building's coming apart faster than the soles of my skateboarding shoes—it's practically falling down around us.

But don't let that concern you, 'cuz you and I have other things to focus on now that we're teaming up again. I'm talking, of course, about the next phase of your complete and total middle school domination: running for class president.

You've already proved you're a total boss, so now it's

time to actually become one. Once you're president, you'll have powers beyond your wildest dreams. You can decide the theme for the school dance. And pick the location for the class field trip. And force all the teachers to dump mashed potatoes on their heads and run around the cafeteria clucking like chickens!

OK, maybe not that last part, but it's still pretty dope.

Plus, as the new student, you're exactly the dose of fresh air this institution needs. And, as your advisor, I'll have your back every step of the way.

See, unlike those other so-called "campaign managers," I'll do *anything* to get you elected. I'll use every trick, scheme, and maneuver in the book to win votes. With my expertise, you won't just become president, you'll enjoy a landslide victory!

Now, I will warn you in advance: Just like last time, there *are* some elements of risk involved with my method. However, you gotta break a few eggs to make an omelet. Plus, the election's only four days from today, so we're gonna have to hustle. Unless, of course, you'd prefer to share last place with the *fringe* candidates who have no hope of winning?

Yeah, I didn't think so.

So come on—we better get started. Step into our head-quarters and let's review your killer campaign.

CHAPTER TWO
The Killer Campaign

While the new blood may be unfamiliar, there's at least one kid I'm sure you'll remember: my assistant, Lewis, the greatest second-in-command who ever lived!

Ew, he really needs to fire his gastroenterologist.

Anyway, back to your presidential bid. Before you can even think about running, you're gonna need an agenda—an engaging topic to base your campaign around that'll fire up the voters and keep your name in the spotlight. And I have just the issue: gum in the classroom.

It's the perfect talking point. See, all kids love gum, but the teachers have completely banned it from the premises. Which is ridiculous, 'cuz, other than the odd cavity here and there, it's totally harmless. In fact, studies have shown it can improve test scores, fight hunger cravings, reduce stress, and even help make friends!

Well, you're gonna be the person who finally legalizes it.

As the pro-gum candidate, you'll run on a platform that ensures that every student between here and the drama club has the freedom to chew wherever he or she pleases. Blowing bubbles won't just be a privilege in this school but an inalienable *right*.

To assist with getting your message out and securing your victory, I've created the patent-pending Max Corrigan Nine-Point Ultimate Presidential Plan. It has, naturally, nine essential components:

The first is a *campaign announcement*. To rally your base and generate buzz, you'll make a grand speech declaring your run for office and your total awesomeness.

. . . and, for these reasons, the New Kid has decided to enter the race.

The second step is *advertising*. With some well-placed ads, we can increase your awareness and drive

This episode has been sponsored by The New Kid for President: the best choice for William H. Taft Middle School.

your message home through constant media exposure.

For some extra fire-power, we go after *endorsements.* If you can get a big-name school celeb to vouch for you, all of his or her followers will be lining up on Election Day to put you in office.

Then you've got the *press.* By getting some sick articles about your campaign in newspapers and blogs, you can change the hearts and minds of even the staunchest critics.

Up next, I'd suggest some good old-fashioned *information gathering.* Whatever you can learn about your opponents will go a long way toward ensuring you're one step ahead of the pack rather than two steps behind.

Try this bubble gum and **tell me** it shouldn't be allowed in school.

FREE!

Sixth on the list is *swag*. If we can put your issue directly into people's hands for them to touch and experience, it'll be far more real to them. The votes will come pouring down like soda into a Big Gulp.

Speaking of Big Gulps, if you really want your message swallowed up by the masses, nothing's more unifying than a catchy *campaign song*. With the right jingle, the school will be singing your tune as they cast their ballots.

Can't get the New Kid out of my head. So good!

. . . and that's why gum—and the New Kid—are clearly the right choice for this school.

The eighth component is a *debate*. If you can defeat your rivals through a spirited discussion, you'll demonstrate just how superior a candidate you are. There's no *debating* how effective that can be.

Last on the list is *reputation*. By showing the voters your history of getting things done, no one will be able to deny that you're a hero while all your opponents are zeros. What else is there to say?

I believe my candidate's record speaks for itself.

Since an epic *announcement* is the first thing you'll need to launch your campaign, we should start with that. Unfortunately, the written word and I aren't really the best of buds. I tried drafting your campaign speech last night, and this is the best I could come up with:

Hello. I am running 4 president. Do u like presidents? Then u should vote 4 me. K? Thanks!

However, I do know an amazing wordsmith who can write your speech for you. And her name is Kenisha Chapman.

Kenisha is the school's best writer. She's so legit her stories have been published in the school paper, kid lit blogs, and even *Highlights* magazine! If you can get her to draft your announcement, you'll be made in the shade! And, as luck would have it, she's in the library with your language arts class right now.

So let's head over there immediately and try to convince her! I can't wait to announce your campaign—something tells me this first chapter of your political story is gonna be a real page-turner.

CHAPTER THREE

Library Carded

Or it could be as dull as a twelve-hour road trip to a turnip farm. Oh my God, I can barely stay awake. Seriously, doctors could prescribe this as a cure for insomnia.

But thankfully *you* did the reading. 'Cuz if you hadn't, Kenisha Chapman would certainly give you a one-star review.

She's such a bibliophile, she even reads the parts that come *after* the novel's over!

Did you know that Hemingway wrote this as a reaction to criticism for *Across the River and into the Trees*?

It says so **deep in the appendix**.

Wait. You *have* read *The Old Man and the Sea*, haven't you?

You haven't?

Uh-oh, that's not good! If you're busted in front of Kenisha, she'll never agree to write your speech! We gotta do something quick before you're called on to talk about it!

Don't sweat it, I can help—that's what I'm here for, remember? And I've got the perfect solution to your reading conundrum. It's a time-honored technique employed by only the *smartest* and *most cunning* people around. I'm referring to an *ingenious* method of acquiring *vast literary knowledge* in the span of mere *minutes*.

You're gonna fake it.

Look, I know fake-reading a book might seem hard, but you're talking to a guy who aced his language arts class last year, and the only thing I read had word balloons and pictures of men in capes fighting other men in capes. I got this.

So grab your bookmarks, 'cuz I'm gonna show you . . .

HOW TO FAKE YOUR WAY THROUGH ANY BOOK

There are a lot of boring books in the world, and for some strange reason, teachers want you to read 'em all. Here's how to convince them you've scrutinized a novel without ever having read a single word.

EXPLORE THE ALTERNATIVES

You don't have to read a book to know what's up. If you've got time, surf the Internet and check out summaries from

Wikipedia, CliffsNotes, or SparkNotes. Or, better still, watch the movie version and enjoy the book the way it was meant to be experienced: on the big screen!

JUDGE A BOOK BY ITS COVER (AND INTERIOR)

Bringing in a pristine copy of a novel to class is a dead give-away that you haven't read it. Instead, fool your teachers by making the book look like you've devoured it a billion times over. Scuff it up. Dog-ear pages. Highlight random phrases and write enigmatic notes in the margins. If done correctly, your book should look like it's been to war and back!

No way this thing's ever been read.

Clearly been devoured.

AVOID SPECIFICS

Don't let the details trip you up. When talking about the story, speak as generally as possible and avoid characters' names, plot points, or anything else that could give you away. To add to the subterfuge, throw in a lot of random literary words like *foreshadowing*, *dramatic irony*, and *catharsis*. Your teachers will think you totally know what you're talking about when, in reality, you're speaking straight out of the place where the sun don't shine.

I loved the **climax**. I could barely put the book down while reading it! Enthralling!

The **denouement** was moving. Not entirely perfect, but emotionally satisfying.

The **protagonist** was complicated, you know? But also simple, when you really reflect on it.

There were a lot of **struggles** in this story— man vs. man, man vs. himself, man vs. this book.

Heh, that last one's a joke.

LIFESAVING LITERARY WORDS

plot, structure, denouement, antihero, antagonist, protagonist, catharsis, characterization, conflict, dialogue, dramatic irony, foreshadowing, critique, symbolism, tragic flaw, analogy, metaphor, archetype, climax, motif

DEFLECT, DEFLECT, DEFLECT

If you're pressed for details by a particularly persistent teacher, deflect the interrogation by changing the subject to something you *do* know about. I like to relate a personal anecdote. That way, people think I have an honest-to-goodness connection with the book when, the truth is, I've never read a single page. Works like a dream!

ASK THE QUESTIONS YOURSELF

Finally, why wait to get caught? Turn the tables by asking the questions *yourself*! You'll gain crucial information *and* make it seem like you actually care about the book! It's a win-win!

Need to finish a book fast and don't want to _entirely_ fake it? Try these

LIGHTNING-FAST SPEED-READING TECHNIQUES FOR THE BUSY MIDDLE SCHOOLER

ONLY READ THE FIRST AND LAST PARAGRAPH OF EACH PAGE
You'll skip tons of useless words and your mind will piece the rest together!

READ EVERY OTHER CHAPTER
You can figure out what happened in between. It's like going to the bathroom while watching a movie. You didn't miss nothin'!

START AT THE END
Read the ending _first_ and work your way _backward._ That way, if you don't have time to finish, you already know how the story shakes out!

ONLY FOCUS ON THE PLOT
Ignore all descriptions and only focus on the plot. Unless something seems important, ditch it and move on!

All right, I've made you a literary know-it-all. Now fake your way through the book and talk to Kenisha after class. Let's pray your story adds up. 'Cuz if you don't impress her, your political career might *not* have a happy ending.

CHAPTER FOUR

Good Reads

That thing you said in class about the overarching themes? Amazeballs. And your analysis of the plot? So good. I thought I knew everything there was to know about *The Old Man and the Sea*, but you've clearly read the novel a few more times than I have.

So you're looking for a speechwriter, huh? Considering

your vast literary knowledge, I think you'd be more than qualified to do it yourself. But, if it's another hand you want, I'm happy to come up with some inspiring words.

The only problem is, I don't know if I've got the time. I'm already overwhelmed writing my current novel. I've been working on it for a year and it's almost finished!

It's about a regular kid who discovers he's actually the prince of the lost world of Atlantis by decoding secret messages hidden in his homework!

THE ATLANTIS PAPERS
By Kenisha Chapman

However, I might be able to put it aside if you can help me out with something. See, much like Finneas Gilligan, the main character of my story, I have issues. And my most pressing one right now is the school book club.

Our club is the bomb. Unfortunately, at the moment, it's a stink bomb. That's because we've read virtually every book in the library already. Twice. And the school says, due to budget cuts, they don't have the money to purchase new ones. And if we don't get some fresh novels on our reading list soon, we'll have nothing else to talk about. We'll have to disband!

But maybe you can do something about that?

As class president, you'll have a lot of influence. If you promise to get us some new books when you're elected, I'd totally be down to help you. In fact, I'll even throw in a couple of deep metaphors about gum that'll hit kids right in the stomach, where it counts. Your campaign will be off to a flying start!

So how about it? Agree to back us when you're in power, and I'll whip out your announcement right now. 'Cuz I think, together, you and I could craft a wonderful narrative.

CHAPTER FIVE

Some Not-So-Friendly Competition

Speaking of sick, that backroom deal you just made was pretty sick itself! I knew you had it in you! It's just like old times—Max and the New Kid, taking names and kicking butt! And now that you've got your speech, I know just where to deliver it. Follow me.

Hey, it pays to understand people's weaknesses!

Anyway, you're good to go. Lay your speech down on that mic and drop it like it's hot! The kids are gonna love you!

What'd I say? You're a political *beast!* Between my skills and your resourcefulness, you've got this election locked up. There's not a person in this school who could keep you from winning the presidency!

Oh, shoot, I forgot about him. Austin Marchman. He's running for class president, too. He's part of a political dynasty—his father, grandfather, and great-grandfather all held the position when they were students here. The kid is loaded—his dad invested in selfie sticks when they were just a piece of wood and a rubber band, and now he's worth a fortune. And Austin's using his vast wealth to buy every vote he can. I mean, listen to his campaign speech!

Sure, it might sound good to the average voter, but Austin could care less about the school's problems—he's only out for himself! If he had his way, he'd slash the budget even more! Art supplies would be reduced! The charity car wash would be canceled! He'd ruin this school! And all because he thinks every kid could have his advantages if only they tried harder. But that entitled moneybags has never worked a day in his life!

Whoever Austin's campaign manager is, he must be one crafty sneak to get students to swallow his awful plans. I can just picture him, too—some alpha bro with rippling muscles and a wispy mustache who's all about winning at any cost. A real stone-cold, hairy-knuckled *brute*.

Wow. I can't believe it's Hailee. I haven't seen her since Camp Thunderbird. We hung out all summer. But she was shorter then and her hair was a lot . . . less *shiny*.

Ugh. Can you believe these guys? Tell me they don't make you want to pluck out your eyelashes.

Son of a—! Those audacious little—!

If that one-percenter and his campaign manager think we can just be brushed off like a bunch of dirty crumbs, they've got another thing coming. We've got to do something to let them know we're serious competitors!

I know: Deface Austin's campaign poster! It'll totally bring them down a peg or two!

Yes, it's like I always say, "When the going gets tough, the tough get vandalizing." It's the classic answer to so many of life's little problems. Which is good, 'cuz the last thing we need is any more trouble on the road to your political victory.

Aw, nards.

CHAPTER SIX

The Vice Principal's Principles

I don't think we've been formally introduced yet. I'm Vice Principal Hartley. It's a pleasure to finally sit down and talk with you.

I hope you didn't think I was going to yell at you for what you did back there. Heavens, no! See, unlike Principal Sitz, I believe that middle schoolers should have the freedom to express themselves however they choose. From a catchy song to a spirited painting, there are so many wonderful ways for students to engage with their feelings. I, myself, like to knit.

I would just urge you to be more mindful of your message in the future so as not to upset the other students.

Speaking of which, I heard you announce that you were running for class president. I applaud your interest in school politics. It's quite commendable.

I do wonder, though, if you're absolutely certain you

want to run? I know Max makes it sound enjoyable, but it's actually a lot of work. Plus, the vast majority of students are already behind Austin Marchman. He's an upstanding young man, and I'd hate to see the school divided by unnecessary competition. Especially considering all the other challenges we're facing with the budget cuts.

If you'd like to reconsider, you'd have my full support. Maybe I could give you a free period to play sports, read a book, or anything else you'd like. I might even run out to get you a cookie from the cafeteria. It's something I always do for students who come to me with problems.

Anyway, it was really nice sharing this special moment with you. Now go on and enjoy the rest of your day. And maybe even get some learning done in between all the hijinks and fun.

Do you want a hug before you leave?

CHAPTER SEVEN

Something Rotten

Oh man, I'm so sorry I got you in trouble with the vice principal! What happened in there, anyway? She didn't threaten to lock you up and throw away the key, did she? I mean, she wouldn't. She's a total softie, right? *Right?*

Seriously, what happened?

Nice! See, what'd I tell you? Total softie. Not like my dad. Which is good news.

Not good news, though, is Austin Marchman. If he ends up as class president, it could be deadlier for this school than that time Vinnie Cutler hid his egg salad sandwich in the heating vent and forgot about it for a week! They had to call in the CDC 'cuz everyone was so sick from the smell!

And with Hailee as Austin's campaign manager, things are only gonna get stinkier. 'Cuz, despite her silky hair, honey-tinged voice, and a smile that you could just live inside of . . .

And let's not forget about those earlobes. Those cute little earlobes . . .

What? No, I **don't** like her! I just appreciate a good face, is all!

Anyway, what I meant to say was, despite all that, she doesn't play around. That means we're gonna have to kick it up a notch to win. 'Cuz if you lose and Austin gains power, it won't just be your reputation that gets wrecked—it'll be the entire school.

Meet me tomorrow morning at HQ and bring your A game. Starting then . . .

. . . your campaign's about to get *real.*

TUESDAY

CHAPTER EIGHT

Breaking the Internet

Hope you had a restful night! Since we last spoke, my staff's been hard at work on your campaign. Lewis even canvassed the school, doing some informal polling, and he's got great news!

Ew, just be glad he didn't say number *three*. I don't even want to *know* what that is.

Anyway, while Lewis's info isn't exactly music to my nose, it *is* music to my ears. Thanks to your epic announcement yesterday, you're closing in on Austin's lead. Now we just need to obliterate it.

And we can start doing that with the second component of my presidential plan: *advertising*. By creating some dope ads, we can drive your message home and show voters that you're clearly the best candidate for the job.

Of course, a few simple posters plastered around the hallways won't cut it against masters of the game like Austin and Hailee—not in this day and age, when video is king.

No, if your advertising is gonna be effective, it's gotta

be filmed and shared on the Internet. I'm talking about making a viral video!

It's the ideal marketing tactic! Viral videos are cheap, easy to produce, and grab more eyeballs than a demented optometrist! If we can upload your video to a popular channel, it'll be guaranteed to take off.

And the kid who's gonna help with that is Lester Vilarrasa.

Lester's the head of the film society and the school's best videographer. His YouTube channel, Choking on Laughter, is the most hilarious thing to hit the Internet since the invention of Rickrolling—*everyone* in William H. Taft Middle School watches it.

If we can get Lester to upload your viral ad to his channel, you couldn't ask for better exposure!

Unfortunately, Lester's a tough critic—he doesn't put just *anything* on Choking on Laughter. To get his stamp of approval, you've got to come up with material so infectious it could break the Internet. And you'd need a promotional strategy to go with it, too, so Lester knows you're legit. And that's easier said than done.

Fortunately for you, I've filmed a few viral sensations in the past. Or have you never witnessed any of my famous Doctor Kitten videos?

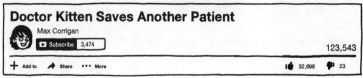

I can help you shoot some clips that are bound to tear through the web. So put your phone on record and follow me, 'cuz I'm gonna teach you . . .

Action!

HOW TO MAKE A VIDEO THAT'S MORE VIRAL THAN A CASE OF THE CHICKEN POX

Anybody can make a video and upload it to YouTube. But to make one that spreads faster than an infectious rash at a hugging convention takes work and careful thought. Here's my advice for crafting Internet gold.

PICK A WINNING GENRE

There are tons of different types of Internet videos. To achieve Internet infamy, stick to the genres everyone knows and loves.

Cute

There're just too many of them!

A Roomful of Puppies
Max Corrigan
Subscribe 3,562
142,006
+ Add to ➤ Share ••• More 👍 11,101 👎 0

Talent

Oh, I think that I've found myself a cheerleader . . .

Kid Burps Song "Cheerleader" by OMI
Max Corrigan
Subscribe 3,562
23,987
+ Add to ➤ Share ••• More 👍 8,398 👎 52

Epic fails

Put it out! Put it out!

Chemistry Experiment Goes Horribly Wrong
Max Corrigan
Subscribe 3,562
299,891
+ Add to ➤ Share ••• More 👍 46,015 👎 12

Educational

Now, you want a lot of **suction** in between your hand and armpit . . .

The Secret to Making the Perfect Fake Fart
Max Corrigan
Subscribe 3,562
311,812
+ Add to ➤ Share ••• More 👍 9,971 👎 22

Pranks

Ahhhh!

Brains . . . Brains . . .

Fake Zombie Terrifies Students
Max Corrigan
Subscribe 3,562
787,619
+ Add to ➤ Share ••• More 👍 51,478 👎 38

Stunts

This might not have been the best idea.

Skateboarding the School While Blindfolded
Max Corrigan
Subscribe 3,562
501,007
+ Add to ➤ Share ••• More 👍 20,066 👎 95

KEEP IT SHORT

The best videos on the Internet are crazy short. So limit your running time to just two or three minutes *max*—even quicker, if possible. Then, if it's a hit, you can always release an extended cut!

MAX CORRIGAN
THE CRITERION EDITION

RUNNING TIME: 36 SECONDS

DIRECTOR'S CUT—NOW WITH AN ADDITIONAL 3 SECONDS!

▶ ⏭ 🔊 0:00 / 0:36   cc ✿ ▭ ▢ ⟨⟩

THE POWER OF THE
MASH-UP

For epic page views, try combining genres to make something totally wicked. After all, if people love cute things and stunts, then they'll lose their you-know-what over a cute thing that *also* does stunts! It's simple math!

Tell me you wouldn't watch this a million times.

GIVE IT A TITLE THAT MAKES PEOPLE WANT TO CLICK ON IT

My Singing Dog is a perfectly fine title. However, Dog Sings Classical Opera—You Won't Believe How Its Owner Reacts! is a zillion times better! Entice viewers by giving your video a catchy heading that hooks their curiosity. Use these awesome templates to help you get started.

CLICK-BAIT TITLES YOU CAN'T *NOT* CLICK ON

- A _____ Does _____. You Won't Believe What Happens Next!

- This Video of _____ Will Restore Your Faith in Humanity!

- This One Video of _____ Will Change Your Life Forever.

- Here's a Video of _____. The First Minute Made Me _____. The Second Made Me _____.

- Think _____ Is Bad? You Won't After You See This Video!

- This One Video Changed Everything I Thought I Knew About _____.

- Why You Should Always _____.

- Why You Should Never _____.

- Ever Wonder Why _____? This Video Explains It All!

TIME YOUR RELEASE

Time your video's release for maximum exposure. Avoid weekends, holidays, or near the end of the week, when people won't be spending as much time online. Instead, make it public on a Monday or Tuesday morning, when kids will have plenty of time to forward it to their friends. Once Saturday rolls around, your video might just be lighting up the Internet!

PROMOTE, PROMOTE, PROMOTE!

Lastly, market your video like a pro! Share it on YouTube, Vimeo, Facebook, Twitter, Reddit, Digg, StumbleUpon, and any other website you can think of. Talk incessantly about it to anyone who will listen. In order to get massive traffic, you need to think and act like a mini Kardashian.

And . . . cut!

Awesomesauce! That is one boss video you just recorded!

I can see traces of *Charlie Bit My Finger* with a little bit of *David After the Dentist* and some early *Harlem Shake* influences. I'd watch the heck out of that!

And I'm sure Lester Vilarrasa will agree. Let's show him now. Something tells me he's gonna give your ad a major *thumbs-up*.

Look, don't get me wrong—it's a stellar clip. But the camera work leaves a lot to be desired. And the audio doesn't exactly pop. If you're gonna reach the masses, you've got to have some killer production values.

Take my first hit, *Cat Drops Dead Mouse in Owner's Food While He's Not Looking—Hilarity*

Ensues. That didn't just *happen.* I had to film it *four times* to get the right reaction shot. Not to mention, the first time I did it, I accidentally had my camera in portrait mode like a noob. I almost puked from embarrassment!

Anyway, I don't know if I could put this on my channel. You'd need better focus, framing, you name it.

I could see it! I could actually see it!

Tell you what: I might be able to reconsider. But if I'm putting my reputation on the line with your video, I'm gonna need something in return from you. And I know just the favor.

The film society just got this amazing print in of *The Dark Knight*. It's the sickest movie in Chris Nolan's epic trilogy. And seeing it on film rather than digital truly lets you appreciate his cinematic vision.

Unfortunately, the school projector is more broken than my leg was after I fell off my roof trying to capture an overhead aerial shot. The darn thing's eaten the last three movies we've tried to watch!

This is all that's left of *Harry Potter and the Prisoner of Azkaban*.

And the school won't pay for a new projector because of the budget cuts. Yet, somehow, the football team always seems to get new uniforms!

But maybe you can do something about that when you're in office . . .

If you agree to help swing some of that money our way when you're elected, I'll be happy to put your ad on my channel. Not only that, but I'll also list it as a featured video. It'll be the first thing anyone who visits Choking on Laughter sees. You can't ask for better placement!

So, what do you think? Agree to help the film society with our projector issue and I'll make your video a hit.

Shall I press "upload"?

CHAPTER TEN

Impressionable Minds

Mad props! Do you know how hard it is to get a video on Lester's channel? Yet you got it posted like a boss! Total respect. And, thanks to your upload, Austin and Hailee must be downloading in their pants right now. Lewis just texted to say you've gained some major ground!

Although, you've still got a ways to go to catch up. Which means it's time to move on to the next part of my presidential strategy. And I know just the thing to change Austin's tune—*a killer campaign song.*

A memorable campaign song can drive your message home by sticking inside voters' heads. With the right band recording your jam, you'll easily close Austin's lead.

And the sickest band in all of William H. Taft is the Suspensions!

These rockers are so progressive, they invented a whole new style of music called locker-core. Their last record was even featured on *Pitchfork*'s *Best Middle School Albums of All Time!*

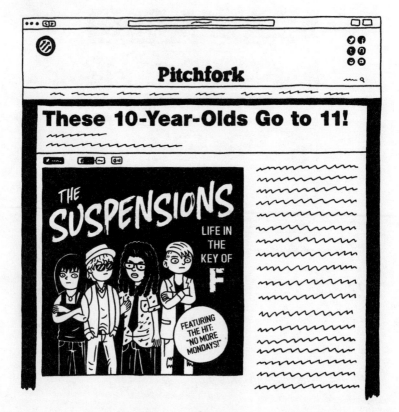

If you can get them to lay down your track, you'll be *unstoppable!*

Unfortunately, there's just one tiny, little, minuscule, eensy-weensy, infinitesimally small problem: The Suspensions only respect other killer musicians. Unless you've been graced by the Rock Gods with the power to shred, wail, or tear, there's no way they'd agree to let you use their tunes. And, believe me, there are very few people good enough to impress these hipsters.

However, there might be a way to convince them you've got the skills to pay the bills without striking a single chord.

If we could get a rock legend to vouch for your musical chops, the Suspensions would totally think you're the real deal and you wouldn't even have to prove it!

And who do the Suspensions love more than the god-father of punk, Iggy Pop. They just discovered his music last year and he's all they talked about in their *Pitchfork* profile! If we could get the man himself to say how amazing you are, you'd totally have it made!

Of course, there's no way we could actually get the *real* Iggy Pop to call the Suspensions. If I had that much juice, I'd be sippin' Shirley Temples on a yacht with Drake right now instead of hanging out in middle school.

However, maybe Iggy Pop doesn't have to call them. Maybe they only need to *think* he has.

If you were to phone up the Suspensions with a killer Iggy impression, I bet they'd totally fall for it! Throw in a few nice words from him about your rock bona fides, and you'd be so in, you'd practically be their fifth member! Tell me that plan doesn't hit the right chords!

Now, for this scheme to work, your impression has to be spot-on. Like, so good it could be on *Saturday Night Live*.

And that takes a certain amount of skill.

Fortunately, I've enrolled in some after-school improv classes at the Upright Students Brigade and can teach you every trick I learned.

So clear your throat and warm up your pipes, 'cuz this is . . .

HOW TO IMPERSONATE ANYONE SO BELIEVABLY EVEN THEIR OWN MOTHER COULDN'T TELL THE DIFFERENCE

Sometimes you have to pretend to be somebody else— whether it's impersonating your parents to call in an unexcused absence, pranking your friends for mondo laughs, or assuming a new identity to flee the country after an illegal deal goes south and some pretty scary goons are hot on your tail. Whatever the case, these tips should help you become an expert mimic.

STUDY UP

No matter what the impersonation, they all start the same: with research. To get the complexities and nuances of your character, commit your subject's physical mannerisms, vocal traits, likes, dislikes, and personal histories to memory. You should know them so thoroughly that you could win a trivia show devoted entirely to them!

MAKE MUSIC

Forget dialogue at the beginning and focus on musicality. Some people drawl in long, deep, slow sentences, while others shout in short, rapid, high-pitched squeaks. Try to match their rhythm, timing, pitch, and tempo *before* the words are added. Once you nail that, the rest will be a cinch!

UNDER THE WEATHER

Trying to fool someone and your impression just isn't cutting it? Tell them that you're under the weather! People never sound like themselves when they're sick, so you can totally use that as an excuse for sounding different! Works like a charm!

Yes, of course this is Samuel L. Jackson. I just have the flu is all.

I picked it up while filming the new Avengers movie. It's gonna be epic!

...choo!

GET PHYSICAL

Physicality is another huge part of doing impressions, 'cuz the way your face changes can totally alter your voice. To get a spot-on impression, mirror your inspiration's facial features. You'd be shocked just how much that can improve your overall impersonation!

Justin Bieber

'Sup, girl?

Jack Black

Now we're rockin'.

Adam Levine

Anyone seen Blake Shelton around here?

LEARN THE LINGO

When you *are* ready to put some words to your imperson-
ations, try to replicate your subject's dialogue choices as
closely as possible. By viewing the world through their eyes
and reacting to it with their unique phrases and pronunci-
ations, your impression will kick so much booty it could be a
professional wrestler!

A **BAD**
ARNOLD SCHWARZENEGGER
IMPRESSION.

You're really doing a great job with those push-ups! Ten is **totally enough!**

A **GOOD**
ARNOLD SCHWARZENEGGER
IMPRESSION.

Yah, you need to git more muscles, you puny human.

You've got to do ze squat thrusts and ze bench presses and ze jumping jacks and such.

Now keep pumping up. 'Cuz if you don't . . .

I'll be back.

PRACTICE MAKES PERFECT

Finally, a good impression takes time. To totally own it, practice over and over again. Record yourself with your phone and study the results. Once you've mastered it, your impression will be so convincing, it'll be impossible to distinguish from the real thing!

Hey, do you know if the Stooges will ever put out another new album, 'cuz my dad would love to—

Oh, I'm sorry—I totally forgot I wasn't talking to Iggy Pop himself! Wow, you really mastered that impression!

Now it's time to unleash it on the Suspensions.

Quickly, give them a call and stop by their class afterward. I only hope you make a favorable impression. 'Cuz if you don't nail it, you might be singing a very sad tune.

CHAPTER ELEVEN

Backstage Pass

This is such a coincidence—you'll never guess who we just got off the phone with! Iggy Pop! Can you believe it? And all he wanted to talk about was you! He said you were a musical genius of the highest order! You must have rock 'n' roll built right into your DNA. Consider us impressed!

Mr. Pop also said you wanted us to record your campaign song. Well, considering the man himself vouches for you, we'd be honored. In fact, we were so inspired by our chat with him that we already started putting together a tune. Check it out!

It's just a demo, but once we flesh it out, it's gonna be hot. And you can totally use it.

There's just one thing we'd love in return.

After a year of jamming, we're finally ready to start laying down some fresh tracks for our new record. It's gonna be a mega-dope concept album that fuses space rock with prog rock, a little bit of R&B, a touch of bluegrass, a healthy dose of '70s-era disco, and a light smattering of metal. We can't wait to get started!

Unfortunately, for something as ambitious as we're planning, we need better equipment—the school's instruments are so busted, animals practically live inside of 'em.

They are kinda cute, though.

And the teachers say there's no way they can fix anything, which is a total bummer, 'cuz without the right instruments, we'll never achieve our vision.

However, as class president, you might be able to figure something out.

If you agree to hook us up with the gear we need once you're in office, we'll totally let you use our song. Not only that, but we'll also play at your victory party. It'll be the illest event that William H. Taft Middle School has ever seen! You'll be the bomb!

So, how about it? Promise to upgrade our equipment when you're prez, and we'll make sure kids sing your praises well past the election.

Chapter Twelve

Tricks of the Trade

I have to say, I'm über-impressed. The way you just struck a deal—it's like you were born with a campaign sticker in your hand! Way to go!

And now that your song's hitting the hallways, it's already catching on with the voters. Listen to how much they're digging it!

And, to make things even better, Lewis just texted to say your numbers are spiking! You're almost neck and neck with Austin!

Now we just need something to push you over the edge. And I know exactly how to make that happen—by bringing out the next component of my grand presidential strategy: *swag*.

Swag is the perfect political aid because it makes your issue *real*. By letting kids touch and taste the thing you're fighting for, your cause will be much more sympathetic. And, since you're struggling to legalize gum in school, it's clear what we need to hand out: G-to-the-U-to-the-M *gum*. If we can find a way to pass out some of those bodacious bubbles, Austin'll be quivering in his penny loafers!

Unfortunately, since gum is hard-core banned, there's no way for me to sneak in enough of it at one time to give to every voter. I'd never be able to get it past security.

However, I do know someone with a massive supply that's totally legit: Mandeep Patel.

Mandeep has a doctor's note that allows him to chew gum wherever he pleases to treat his stress condition. And, since he's a world-class foodie, Mandeep's stash is *amazing!* He has artisanal flavors like maple bacon, jalapeño, and peanut butter cheesecake! They're to die for!

If we can get Mandeep to contribute to your cause, you'll be so close to the presidency, you might as well move into the White House!

But that's not going to happen. At least not easily.

See, Mandeep won't just give his gum away to *anyone*. In order to convince him, you'd have to get on his good side. And the only way to win over a foodie like him is through his belly.

If you hooked Mandeep up with a lunch so scrumptious it could be Michelin rated, it might be enough to get him to part with his goods. But it's seriously gotta be grade-A awesome. Like pizza-straight-from-an-oven-in-Italy tasty!

However, maybe you've already got something in your backpack that fits the bill. What did you bring for lunch, anyway?

Yeah, that's not gonna come anywhere close enough.

But don't worry—you're not cooked yet. I wouldn't be Max Corrigan if I didn't have a plan. And I've got a way to improve your lunch so drastically it won't be just the envy of the cafeteria, but a meal so divine that Mandeep Patel will be drooling all over himself to try it.

You, my friend, are gonna trade up.

Now, I know what you're thinking: Converting a common bag lunch into a five-star meal might seem like a herculean task, but I got your back here. I've done trades in the past so large they were practically listed on the New York Stock Exchange. I can totally hook you up.

So follow me to the cafeteria and grab a lunch tray, 'cuz I'm gonna show you . . .

HOW TO TURN A LUNCH WORTH CRYING OVER INTO A LUNCH WORTH DROOLING OVER

The secret ingredient is deception.

Parents sometimes pack the worst lunches. But a culinary catastrophe can be upgraded to a fantastic feast by using a quarter cup scheming, a few ounces of lies, and a dash of showmanship. These are my favorite schemes for trading up even the grossest food.

USE THE POWER OF "YES"

Yes is the most powerful word in the dictionary. Use it to your advantage by asking potential traders questions they can't help but say yes to. This will automatically put them in a positive frame of mind, and they'll leap at the chance to exchange goods! It totally works!

MAKE UP A STORY

You don't sell the steak, you sell the *sizzle*. To trade your food, attach a story to it that pulls at the heartstrings and grabs people on an emotional level. It won't just be a crummy lunch anymore, it'll be elevated to a powerful symbol every kid will be dying to have!

CHANGE THE PRESENTATION

People eat with their eyes, not with their mouths. Increase your chances of trading by making your food look as appealing as possible. Try these tricks to give your lunch a culinary makeover.

Small food, big plate.

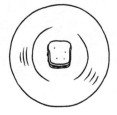

Interesting shapes.

Stacked high.

Drizzled and swirled.

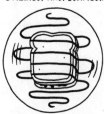

Abstract art.

Accessorized.

MAKE YOUR OPPONENT'S FOOD SEEM LESS APPETIZING

Finally, you can also increase your food value by making your opponent's food seem worse. Point out all the negative things associated with it—even if you're totally just pulling them out of thin air. Once their food seems completely unappetizing, yours will seem like a five-star meal in comparison. They'll be begging to unload theirs!

THE MICROTRADE STRATEGY

Sometimes it's impossible to get everything you want in just one trade. If that's the case, try converting your whole lunch into a single power dish and then doing a series of microtrades afterward to build up to bigger and better things. Check out this chart to see how I'd go from a crummy healthy lunch to a greasy indulgence of the senses.

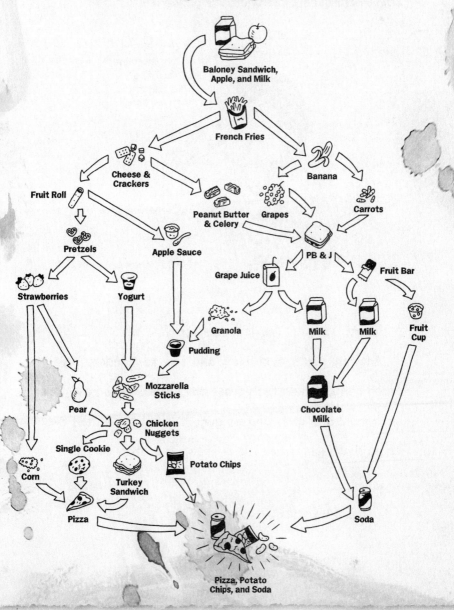

Pizza, Potato Chips, and Soda

Yum, that is one tasty meal you just scored! I can't stop salivating. Of course, that might also be because I got myself some chocolate pudding while you were haggling. And you *know* how much I love chocolate pudding.

Oh, chocolate pudding . . . The things you do to me, baby . . .

What? Don't act like you're better than me!

Anyway, you should hurry and talk to Mandeep before lunch period's over. Let's cross our fingers that he enjoys your meal and gives you his gum. 'Cuz otherwise, the only thing that'll get chewed up will be your political career.

CHAPTER THIRTEEN
TASTY BUDS

Nice work on this tasty meal. You really know your way around a lunch tray. And I don't say that often.

So you'd like to use my gum for your election campaign, huh? While I agree that it should be allowed in school, it's not something I can part with easily.

See, the gum I have is very limited edition. Some of these flavors they don't even make anymore. I mean, you try finding a box of cheddar avocado gum and let me know what you come up with.

Yeah, I didn't think so. (And, by the way, before you judge, it's delicious.)

Still, I like your politics. And us chewers gotta stick together. So maybe we can come to an arrangement. And I know just the thing to ask for.

I'm sure you've seen the Chicken Bake Surprise floating around the cafeteria? It's a blight on the human digestive system that the lunchroom deems fit to serve at least twice a week. No joke, the thing is gross.

Well, I've tried to get it replaced with something less gnarly, but the higher-ups claim it's impossible due to budgetary constraints. And if we don't get some edible food here soon, I'm worried kids are gonna go on a hunger strike. It's seriously stressing me out.

But, as class president, you might be able to sway the powers that be.

If I help you get elected, will you promise to replace the Chicken Bake Surprise with something digestible? With your help, I know we could finally turn the lunch menu around. And, as an added bonus, I'll even serve up the food for your victory party from my mom's organic sweetshop. You'll have so much artisanal candy and fancy chocolate it'll be like twenty Halloweens combined.

So do we have a deal? Agree to get us some better food and I'll go get my gum right now.

CHAPTER FOURTEEN

Keyed Up

Call me an astronaut, 'cuz I'm over the moon about what you just did! Forget running for class president—with skills like that, you could run for president of the United States of America! Heck, you could run for president of the *world*!

And now that you've acquired Mandeep's gum, it should totally put you in the lead! You'll have voters eating out of your hands once we've secretly passed it out!

Dangerous?! Ruin her life?! What are they talking about? Why would anyone think gum is a threat?

Of course—Austin Marchman! That spoiled pain in the you-know-what. He's using fear tactics to prey on kids' worst anxieties to get votes! That's the lowest form of politicking!

Or Jane Cassidy, who chewed so frequently, she got TMJ in her jaw.

It shtill hurtsh to open my mouthsh.

And even adults like Rufus the Janitor. Nice, dependable Rufus who never hurt a fly.

I've scraped so much gum off of desks that I got carpal tunnel syndrome.

Rufus the Janitor! But we're *friends*! I can't believe that Austin bought him off, too! Is the whole school so easily swayed by all of Austin's fancy gifts that they'll believe whatever he says?

That's why I say, if you really want something to unwrap, unwrap this:

Personalized solid-gold key chains for everyone here!

Because, once you vote me into power, you'll have the **keys** to make your dreams come true!

AUSTIN! AUSTIN! AUSTIN!

No. Flippin'. Way. That giveaway! That catchphrase! It's . . .

It's—

Genius? Thanks. Just a little something I came up with this morning. Nice to see you again, Max.

Hailee.

Isn't she the greatest campaign manager in the world?

Ugh. These guys are really getting under my skin.

If that bothers you, I don't think you're gonna want to watch the school TV station today. Austin's commercial's been playing every twenty minutes.

And I'd avoid the radio, too—the Weeknd recorded his campaign song. It's already a number one hit in the UK.

My dad paid for everything. It sure is nice to be rich. #Blessed.

#IWantToThrowUpInMyMouthRightNow. That's so not fair! How's somebody like you supposed to compete against someone like him? You can never match him!

You're not supposed to compete—you're supposed to lose. And you're doing that quite well, I might add.

Now, **that's** something to **chew on**.

Come on, Austin—I believe you have some designer blazers you wanted to hand out to everyone.

They're Mulberry silk. So breathable.

Oh man, they just undercut our entire advertising plan! Everything we've been working for today—gone in a poof!

This is not good. If they keep this up, the closest you'll get to office will be the nurse's office—from getting your butt beaten so badly in the polls! We've got to do something drastic to turn this around.

If we want to win against Austin, we need to get inside his head. Figure out what his weaknesses are.

Unfortunately, a good kid like me can't grasp Austin's mind. The only way to get inside the skull of a villain is to think like a villain. We need someone evil on our side. Someone vile and repugnant whose moral compass is so broken that the needle's completely missing. And there's only one person I know of in this school who fits that bill.

I swore I'd never speak to him again, but there's no other way—he's our only hope. How serious are you about winning?

No joke, this kid is evil incarnate.

All right, then. Come on and follow me—his locker's right around the corner. Prepare yourself, though, because you and I are about to enter the fifth circle of H-E—double hockey sticks . . .

I hope you brought your sunscreen.

CHAPTER FIFTEEN

The Devil You Thought You Knew

It's nice to see you again. Believe it or not, I've been wanting to apologize to you for the longest time.

See, after our last run-in, I did some major soul-searching. And thanks to the help of my therapist, Dr. Derrick Schweitzer, I've moved past all the negative feelings I used to carry with me. He made me understand that my devious acts were really just a way to deal with insecurities. Now when I feel like doing bad, I unpack those emotions, repeat my mantra, and grab my daily Oreos from the vending machine. The black-and-white yin and yang centers me.

Ahhh, that feels better . . .

So you'd like me to help you defeat Austin in the election? I'm sorry, but I can't aid you—my days of scheming and backstabbing are over.

What I will do instead is assist you in becoming a fully realized, happy individual like I am now. Because self-knowledge is the only path to true enlightenment.

So, how about it? Grab my hand and let's walk down this path of friendship together. As equals.

Would you like an Oreo?

CHAPTER SIXTEEN

Through the Looking Glass

Holy frijoles! I don't even know what to say. Has this whole school gone insane? The vice principal's nice! The kids are eating up Austin's clearly diabolical plans! And Kevin Carl's brain has been taken over by some sort of karmic alien! We're through the looking glass here! Black is white! Up is down! Day is night!

I literally cannot deal. I gotta get outta here and re-
group.

Meet me tomorrow at HQ—hopefully, after a good
night's sleep, my head'll be back in the game and I'll know
exactly how to proceed.

WEDNESDAY

CHAPTER SEVENTEEN

Something to Talk About

Sorry, I barely slept a wink. I was tossing and turning all night trying to wrap my head around the election. But at least Kevin Carl showed up nice and early to help. Not that he'll *be* much of it.

Well, *my* truth is, you're boned unless we figure something out. There must be *some way* to close Austin's lead and put you on top. But even Lewis is stumped for an answer on how to do that.

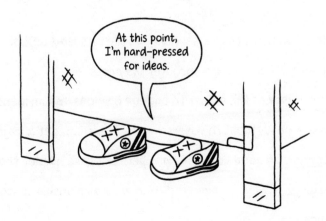

Hold on, that's it! Lewis is a genius! Quick—somebody sugar me up and I'll explain!

Here's how we can chisel away at Austin's lead and bring up your numbers: We go through *the press*!

The press has the power to change opinions and influence even the most stubborn voters' minds. If we can get a major publication on your side, your numbers will spike harder than an Olympic volleyball player during a championship match! It's perfect!

It's just too bad that the *William H. Taft Tattler* has

already given its nod to Austin's campaign—it's the official school paper.

But maybe there's a better rag to sell your story to? An outlet that isn't sanctioned by the school. A bulletin that speaks truth to power. That never compromises. That follows the story wherever it leads, regardless of the consequences!

I'm referring, naturally, to *Chatter Chick*.

Chatter Chick has the biggest gossip blog in school. *Everyone* follows her. She's snarky, irreverent, and totally fearless. She's the one who broke Mr. Rubric's unfair grading policy last year!

If we can get her to sing your praises and denounce Austin's campaign, that'd be an epic win!

However, getting a write-up on Chatter Chick's blog won't exactly be a cinch. In order to sell your story to her, there's got to be an angle to it. A slant—other than running for president—that will hook Chatter Chick's audience. And, I'm sorry to say, that's not something you have right now.

But I think I've got a way around that. We invent it.

If we made you appear so interesting that every aspect of your life seemed ripped from a movie, Chatter Chick couldn't resist writing about you. You'd have your article in no time!

Unfortunately, transforming instantly from ordinary to extraordinary takes work. But, as luck would have it, I can help—I'm a PR *mastermind*. In just a few short minutes, I can make you so intriguing that every kid in this building will want to know your 411.

So get ready to dazzle and delight, 'cuz I'm gonna show you . . .

HOW TO BE THE MOST INTERESTING PERSON IN SCHOOL (EVEN IF YOU'RE DULLER THAN A DENTIST'S WAITING ROOM)

Think being captivating is hard? Not if you know my secret tips! Here's how to make people think you've got more layers than a Spanish onion.

Create a mystery about yourself that'll have everyone talking.

Carry around obscure books of poetry so you appear **way deep**.

"Accidentally" let an amazing fake secret about yourself slip.

Write misleading, off-the-hook status updates.

Invent fake bands you listen to that sound totally cutting-edge.

Don't tell me you've never heard of the Whispering Ghost Monkey Trio! They're, like, **the best**.

Man, you've got some interesting taste.

Post other people's exotic vacation photos on your Instagram.*

helpmemaxcorrigan   2h

♡ ⬭ ↗

♥ **176 likes**

helpmemaxcorrigan My last trip to Spain. Wish I was back there now. **#onlyliveonce**

*Just make sure their real owners aren't in them!

Whoa! I have to admit, I'm kinda regretting giving you that PR upgrade. 'Cuz now that you're so insanely fascinating, I feel sorta boring in comparison.

But at least it's working. I just sent off your press release to Chatter Chick and she's already responded! Check your messages—let's see what else she has to say!

CHAPTER EIGHTEEN

Email Exchange

Subject: Re: Interview Request

From: Chatter Chick

To: The New Kid

CC: Max Corrigan

Date: Wednesday

New Kid,

Thanks 4 having Max reach out. I have to admit, when I first heard u were running 4 class president, I was like, "Why should I care?" But now that I've learned how interesting u are, I'm all, like, "Hold up. This kid's the real deal."

I'd love to do a full above-the-fold feature on u. Your campaign. Your background. Your platform on gum. The works. 'Cuz I think my readers would flip to know more about u and your amazing story.

However . . . I'd like a favor in return.

Running a gossip blog requires information. And right now the rumor mill's at an all-time low. If I don't get hold of some juicy scoops soon, my ad sales are gonna plummet so deeply, I'll have to switch my website over to a free account like Tumblr or Blogger. And those look so unprofessional, I might as well write captions 4 the yearbook committee instead. At least *they* get free pizza.

However, as class president, u could give me the dirt on school government. If u traded me inside info, I could grow my blog exponentially and become the definitive source of news for all of William H. Taft. My advertising would go through the roof, and I'd never have to worry about my site shutting down!

So, what do u think? Agree to scratch my back by becoming my inside source once you're prez, and I'll scratch yours by writing the most glowing profile you've ever read. The rumors of u winning this election won't just be speculation—they'll be the truth.

Yours,

Chatter Chick

(Written from inside the school. Somewhere.)

CHAPTER NINETEEN

Class Act

Nicely done! Are you sure you weren't a media relations expert in another life? 'Cuz you got skills with the press like a pro.

And check this out: Chatter Chick's already posted your feature! And it's getting *tons* of comments!

Thanks to that article, Lewis says your numbers are skyrocketing—you're nipping right at Austin's ankles!

Now you just need to take a huge bite out of

them. And we can do that with another component of my presidential plan: *celebrity endorsements!*

Celebrity endorsements are the real deal when it comes to political strategies. By getting a famous name to vouch for your campaign, almost every one of his or her fans will be swayed to vote for you, too! You'll have so many followers you won't even know what to do with them! And if it's an A-list celebrity we need, I know exactly the one to woo: Mr. Dawson.

Mr. Dawson is the most popular teacher in school. He's totally *on fleek*. Kids and faculty alike worship him 'cuz he's young, hip, easy on the eyes, and one hundred percent legit.

It just so happens that Mr. Dawson is teaching your science class next period. You could totally talk to him and convince him to help!

There's just one minor hiccup: Mr. Dawson *doesn't usually play favorites—he's nonpartisan.* So we might have to shoot for a B-list celebrity instead, like Edith the Lunch Lady or Security Guard Dan. Although she's a bit salty and he's got that weird ear hair thing, and I'm not sure how well either is gonna play with classrooms in the middle of the school.

Ugh, this is too bad—I wish we could get Mr. Dawson. This situation's stickier than a freshly licked sucker.

Hold on, I think I just had an epiphany!

I know how you can get Mr. Dawson interested in your campaign! You *suck up* to him!

See, any teacher can be swayed by sucking up! If you were to make Mr. Dawson feel like he was the greatest thing since sliced bread, I'd wager all my comic books that he'd be moved enough to help you out. You'd have his endorsement in a heartbeat!

However, for this scheme to work, your sucking up has to be major—like vacuum-level suction. And it can't be obvious either, 'cuz if Mr. Dawson saw through it, he'd brand you a brown-noser for life. And so would the other students. And on a scale of 1 to 10 of terribleness, that would be an 11.

Never fear, though—I'm a master at the art of compliments and flattery. I can teach you how to smooch butt like a pro without anyone being the wiser. (And by the way, on a completely unrelated note, did I tell you how nice you look today? Your top really brings out the sparkling color of your eyes.)

So gather your strongest compliments, 'cuz this is . . .

HOW TO SUCK UP TO YOUR TEACHERS WITHOUT LOOKING LIKE A TOTAL BROWN-NOSER

Sucking up to teachers is a great trick to increasing grades, gaining favors, and enjoying the many other perks of being the classroom favorite. However, most kids do it so transparently that they epically fail. Here's how to fool teachers into believing you think they're number one without coming off like number two.

FIRST IN, LAST OUT

If there's one thing teachers love, it's dedication. And nothing says "There's no place I'd rather be" more than being the first student in the door and the last one to leave. So to increase suck-up points, run like the wind to get to your desk before anyone else and stay until the very last bell. Teachers will think you're über-dedicated when, in reality, you're totally just counting down the clock.

FAKE INTEREST

Sure, class may be boring, but not to your teachers. To get on their good side, pretend to be interested in whatever they're talking about. Nod your head as they speak and look like you're jotting down notes—even if you're actually just thinking about what you're going to have for lunch later. Also, it helps to throw in some subtle "Hmm"s and "Huh"s for good measure, as if you've just had a major realization about something they've said. They'll think they've actually gotten through to you, and you'll quickly get on their Good Kids list.

COMPLIMENT INDIRECTLY

Compliments are the cornerstone of any good suck-up campaign. However, most noobs blow it by saying nice things right to their teachers' faces, which is a dead giveaway! Instead, get around that by complimenting your teachers *indirectly* to their peers. Word will eventually travel back, and your teachers will *never* suspect your true motives!

ASK FOR ADVICE

Another great trick is to ask your teachers for advice about something. It could be about homework, school, or a personal problem. Heck, it could even be *fake!* It doesn't matter! Your teachers will be so flattered that you respect their opinion, they'll never realize they're secretly being sucked up to. That's some next-level manipulation!

SHARE A PASSION

A final great way to melt teachers' hearts is to share in their favorite passions. Do some research and find out your teachers' hobbies, interests, and activities. Then, show them that you, too, coincidentally, enjoy the same thing! You'll win major points, and they won't suspect that it's all part of a grand suck-up scheme!

Need to slather on some indirect compliments but don't know where to start? Try these

Guaranteed Suck-up Phrases That'll Totally Win Over Your Teachers

- "For the first time in my life, I finally understand [class subject] thanks to [teacher's name]! No one's ever been able to teach me that before!"

- "[Teacher's name] somehow seems to make class both educational and fun! I didn't even know that was possible!"

- "I wish [teacher's name] was my parent."

- "Whatever they're paying [teacher's name], they need to double it! No—triple it! [Teacher's name] is worth way more than what [he/she] is getting!"

- "In a perfect world, [teacher's name] would teach all of my classes!"

- "I'm not saying that [teacher's name] is the coolest person on earth. I'm just saying that [teacher's name] could give Channing Tatum a run for his money."

- "I always hated school until I had [teacher's name]'s class. Now school is better than fireworks, roller coasters, robots, and double-chocolate brownies combined!"

Sweet, I've turned you into a butt-kissing, compliment-giving machine! Now go out there and suck up to Mr. Dawson as if your life depended on it. I'll see you after his class. Let's just hope he doesn't see through your smoke and mirrors.

I just wanted to say that you really killed it today. I had no idea how much my class meant to you before, but after this morning, I'm seeing you in a whole new light. Don't tell any of the other students, but you just might be my favorite.

Look, I never get involved in politics, but I heard through the grapevine that you could use a boost for your presidential campaign. Well, as it happens, I could pull some strings, 'cuz that's the kinda guy I am.

See, the reason all the students think I'm so dope is 'cuz I *get it*. I know everything you kids are into and I'm down with it all. Because, to be the cool teacher, you've got to be in touch, and speak the lingo, and know the latest trends, and references, and—

I'm sorry, but I can't keep up the charade any longer! I'm not cool and I never was. It's not skateboarding and extreme sports I'm into, it's isotopes and periodic tables. I mean, hello-o-o-o, I'm a *science teacher*!

All of this popular stuff is just an act to keep the students engaged. I have no clue what kids really like. I tried playing *Minecraft* once, but it was just a bunch of blocks! *Blocks!*

I wish I could capture the students' attention with just science alone, but it's impossible. I mean, how am I supposed to do anything cool with outdated equipment like this?

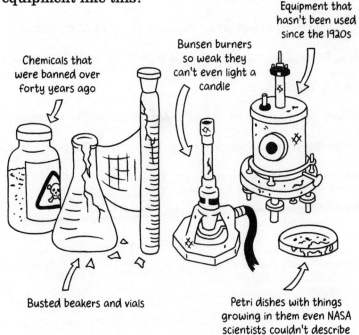

Equipment that hasn't been used since the 1920s

Bunsen burners so weak they can't even light a candle

Chemicals that were banned over forty years ago

Busted beakers and vials

Petri dishes with things growing in them even NASA scientists couldn't describe

And I'm barely holding on. Sooner or later, the kids are going to realize I'm faking it, and then class participation will decay faster than ununoctium, which is the fastest-decaying element known to man!

But maybe you could do something about that?

As the leader of the school, kids would look up to you. If you could champion science and preach how awesome it is once you're elected, they'd totally get behind it without me having to pretend to be hip anymore. I could stop faking it, and the students would still learn! For a deal like that, you'd have my full endorsement.

So, what do you think? Agree to make science a priority during your term, and I'll talk you up to every kid with an eardrum. Your campaign will soar farther than the *Voyager 1* space probe.

CHAPTER TWENTY-ONE

A Sticky Situation

Wow, I had no idea Mr. Dawson wasn't as cool as he was letting on! It really makes you think: Does anybody truly know anyone else? Are human hearts and minds just mysteries we fool ourselves into believing we understand, when, in reality, our fundamental grasp of them is as fleeting as a star burning in the cosmos, alight in its own dwindling energy, pulsing as it slowly vanishes into—

Sorry! Sorry! I get philosophical sometimes. Here's another heavy thought: What if everyone's faces were actually where their butts were instead? Can you imagine what pants would look like!

Anyway, speaking of faces to butts, that butt-kissing you did was more classic than a 1957 Ford Fairlane convertible! Because of your suck-up skills, Mr. Dawson's already spreading your gospel to the students in his next period. Your numbers are bound to go up! I just need to check in with Lewis to see how you're doing and—

Oh no! Lewis just alerted me to a late-breaking story!

Apparently, somebody spat out chewing gum all over the hallways! Kids have been stepping in it for the last ten minutes! It's a nightmare! They're calling it Gumgate!

This is not good—your whole campaign is based around gum! Something like this could rock it to its core! Who could have done such a horrible thing?

Ladies and gentlemen, a tragedy like this is the exact reason why the New Kid can't be president.

Stick with Austin Marchman. I won't just keep these hallways **clean**, I'll give everybody **brand-new sneakers** to make up for this!

Vote Austin Marchman and your **feet** will be **sweet**!

I should have guessed. Austin and Hailee. This is a play right from their strategy book! And, if it works, your campaign is gonna be toast!

We've gotta get back to HQ and put out this fire fast. Come on, follow me. Thank God that Kevin Carl will be waiting for us. An evil genius like him will know exactly what measures to take.

Great. Guess *that's* not gonna happen.

But we've still got to do *something*, 'cuz the media just landed outside. If you don't address this situation now, public opinion will turn on you so fast you won't know what hit you!

Shoot! Think, Max! Think!

OK, what if we pretended it was some kind of contest, right? And everyone who stepped in gum was the lucky winner of a trip to the Bahamas! Or maybe we say that it wasn't even gum at all, but some kind of alien refuse and the school's secretly been invaded by otherworldly life forms! Although we can't really afford to send anyone on vacation, and I don't think people will buy our alien story.

OK, wait, I've got a better idea. I know what we need to do to fix this situation: We spin it.

See, any bad situation can be made to look better under the right light. With the correct spin, we can totally turn this gum travesty around!

Now, spinning things to your advantage is a delicate act and not for the faint of heart. However, I wouldn't be a great campaign manager if I didn't know how to do that. So take notes, 'cuz I'm gonna teach you everything you need to turn lemons into lemonade.

HOW TO SPIN EVEN THE WORST NEWS SO THAT YOU COME OUT SMELLING LIKE A ROSE

Bad stuff happens all the time—whether it's failing a test or accidentally breaking your parents' favorite ceramic kitten sculpture. Here's my advice for skewing the details so that you can get out of trouble scot-free, no matter what the situation.

Choose your words **very** carefully.

It's simply not true. There was no **chewing gum** stuck to anybody's shoes.

That's 'cuz, once it's on the floor, you can't chew it. It's now **floor gum**.

Cherry-pick the facts to make your case look better.

The numbers have been completely blown out of proportion. Only seven men and women were affected by this.

Of course, forty boys and girls were affected, too.

Shift the blame.

Gum isn't responsible anyway—it's the chewers who didn't dispose of it properly. And we'll find and punish them.

Point out all the ways it could be worse.

At least it wasn't in people's hair. Now, **that** would have been a real tragedy.

Make it seem like a positive.

Besides, people should **love** getting gum on their shoes. It's the latest trend in Paris. I actually just gummed up my sneakers myself. *Très chic!*

Sound apologetic without actually apologizing.

Look, clearly mistakes were made. If anyone was hurt in this incident, I would sincerely apologize.

Divert attention.

Can we forget about this distraction and get back to the real issue at hand—what's gonna be the theme for the school dance?

Bury the story by offering up the details when no one's paying attention.

In conclusion, I'll present a full account of our role in this situation on Saturday at eleven p.m. Be sure to listen to your AM radio.

DOUBLESPEAK

Got something unpleasant to say and need to make it sound better? Try using doublespeak! That's where you substitute positive expressions for all your negative words! Here are some of my favorite phrases to use:

ORIGINAL WORDS	DOUBLESPEAK VERSION
Failing grade	Growth-compatible knowledge assessment
Detention	After-hours supervised learning session
Suspension	Home-designated school vacation
Skipping class	Off-campus independent learning experience
Food fight	Aerial food-sharing program
Late to class	Time-sensitive classroom deployment
Lie	Creative alternate truth
Cheat	Easily facilitated fact acquisition
Steal	Self-initiated redistribution of property
Puke	Reverse-eating exchange
Fart	Wind-powered fragrance emission
Passing notes	Impromptu written exchange of ideas
Trip/Fall	Horizontal mobility intensive
Cry	Optical water release
Fight	Spirited physical debate

All right, you're now a master of spin! Go out there and address the public. And remember to smile. Let's hope they buy your take, 'cuz if you don't change the school's perceptions ASAP, your campaign is gonna be DOA.

—

CHAPTER TWENTY-TWO

Up for Debate

Wow, we shouldn't have jumped to conclusions before all the facts were in!

Yeah, after that speech, I'm totally rethinking my stance on this gum scenario.

Not a problem guys. Have a stick on me.

And remember to vote for the New Kid for class president.

Whew! That was *close*. But you did it! In fact, because of your epic spin, I think your numbers may have even gone *up* a little bit after that episode. No thanks to Austin, of course. When I see that bag of wind, I swear to God I'm gonna—

Do what? Get upset?

I had nothing to do with that gum incident. It was a terrible travesty.

Austin denies all responsibility and was just as shocked as you were to hear about it.

Grrrrr . . .

No way! He's lying! And you want to know how I know? 'Cuz his lips are moving! He's a total politician through and through—all flash, no substance!

You know what? Hailee's right! We should solve this civilly—with *words*! Let's put all our cards on the table and talk about the issues! Let the people decide who's right.

Let's have a real, live, actual *debate*!

Good. Then name the time and place.

All right, I'm gonna go prepare. Meet me bright and early at HQ and grab some aspirin—Austin and Hailee will need it for the amount of pain they'll be in after we're done with 'em.

THURSDAY

CHAPTER TWENTY-THREE
Convincing Arguments

Morning. Hope you're ready to do battle, 'cuz *public debates* are like going to war.

A good debate can turn the tide in any political campaign. By putting your arguments in front of the school, you can demonstrate that you're clearly the superior candidate for the job while your opponents are just full of hot air. It's one of the most important factors voters use in determining the winners and losers of an election.

And Austin is about to become the biggest loser this school's ever seen. Because with an evil genius like Kevin Carl behind us, the debate will be a cinch. We just need to unlock his devious power.

Darn it! We almost had him!

Remember: The world is only what you give back to it.

Now, I must get my daily Oreos.

Man, I don't know what his therapist did to him, but it might be permanent.

Not to worry, though—I have my own tactics when it comes to linguistic battles. And my methods are so effective, Austin will never see them coming.

So pay attention, 'cuz this is . . .

HOW TO WIN ANY ARGUMENT, DISAGREEMENT, OR DEBATE—EVEN IF YOU'RE ONE HUNDRED PERCENT WRONG

Disagreements happen all the time—whether it's your parents telling you to go to bed when you're not even tired or some kid in class who thinks they know way more than you about SpongeBob. (As if!) However, by using these kick–butt techniques, you can annihilate even the most skilled debater in the field of battle.

USE CONFIDENCE TO STEAMROLL THEIR ARGUMENTS

People don't listen to the smartest person in the room, they listen to the most confident. So shove your opinions down your opponent's throat with total bravado, even if you have no clue what you're actually talking about. Your opponent will seem totally unsure, and you'll come off like a legit expert in comparison.

. . . and that's why gum should stay illegal in school.

Please, are you gonna take **his** word over **mine**? I've been chewing gum since before I had **teeth**. I was born with a **Juicy Fruit** in my hand.

So I think I know **a little bit more** than my opponent when it comes to gum.

THROW IN FACTS TO MAKE YOUR CASE AIRTIGHT

The great thing about facts is that they're irrefutable. However, not all facts are created equal. Pick and choose yours to present only the ones that support your case, conveniently skipping over any evidence that doesn't. And, if you don't know any facts, just make 'em up! (And remember to stay confident!) Then, move on before your opponent has time to check or refute them. Your argument will seem more solid than a rock!

PLANT DOUBT TO MESS WITH YOUR OPPONENT'S HEAD

You can easily throw off your opponent by making them question their own judgment. Plant doubt by reminding them of other times they've been wrong, made bad decisions, or totally boned it. Once the seed of doubt has started growing and their credibility is chipped away, your argument will seem far sounder than theirs.

EXAGGERATE YOUR OPPONENT'S POSITION TO MAKE THEM SEEM LIKE A RAVING LUNATIC

Here's a great trick: Whatever your opponent says, blow it completely out of proportion. By exaggerating their position to the ultimate extreme, they'll come off like a tinfoil hat—wearing crackpot and you'll come off like the totally sane person you are. You'll be ready to do your victory lap in no time!

NEVER ADMIT DEFEAT, NO MATTER HOW BAD IT LOOKS

Finally, when all else fails, never admit defeat. Ever. No matter how bad it looks, your opponent can't win if you don't concede. And, by not conceding, your argument will still have crazy power. And that's a victory in and of itself!

Arguing isn't just a battle of words—it's an intense mind game. To win before you've even started, try psyching your opponent out. They'll be so thrown off, you'll clobber them without barely having to utter a sentence!

MAX'S ULTIMATE PSYCH-OUTS

Wear a T-shirt with a photo of their mother on it.
It'll make them feel like their parents are judging everything they say!

Add lifts to your shoes to make you seem taller than you actually are.
The bigger you look, the more intimidating you become!

Subtly mispronounce their name every time you say it.
It'll seem like you barely consider them a threat because you hardly know who they are!

Instead of looking at their face when you talk to them, look at their crotch.
They'll become so confused and self-conscious, they won't be able to focus!

Laugh at every point they make.
The funnier they seem to you, the more flustered they'll get!

Give them a hug before you begin.
It'll make them feel bad for disagreeing with you!

All right, your tongue now holds the heat of a thousand suns. Let's head over to the debate.

Now get up there and slaughter him. I can't *wait* to see Austin's reaction when he loses. He won't know *what* hit him.

CHAPTER TWENTY-FOUR
Poking the Bear

That wasn't a debate—that was a series of dirty mind games! You deceitful invertebrate! How dare you sully the March-man name with your tricks!

You might have won this round, but this election is far from over. I won't forget this. And, mark my words, I will do *everything* in my power to make sure I'm class president.

So watch your back. Because now that you've poked the bear, the teeth are coming out.

CHAPTER TWENTY-FIVE
Spy vs. Spy

Ah-ha-ha-ha-ha-ha! That was *classic!* Thanks to your dope debating skills, Austin totally got served! I could watch a video of that over and over! Which is good, 'cuz I recorded it!

And because of his loss, you're finally tied! Let's step back into HQ to review the next steps. Now that we've caught up to Austin, it's time to beat him once and for all and make sure he loses so badly that—

Oh no, it can't be!

I can't believe it! Austin must have broken in just after we saw him! He took everything. My files! My notes! It looks like even Lewis got jacked!

This is espionage of the highest degree. Thank goodness Kevin Carl just arrived. He'll help us!

And there he goes.

And so has my patience.

That rich, arrogant wet blanket Austin has messed with us for the last time. If he really wants to fight dirty, then we're going to see just how dirty he really is. We're going to use another one of my political strategies: *information gathering.*

See, every politician has secrets. And a candidate like Austin must have skeletons in his closet so large they could be dinosaur bones! If we went all *James Bond* on his butt, I bet we would uncover something so heinous we could finally put his campaign in the ground and secure your victory once and for all.

However, before you start investigating, you better hold on. If Austin gets one whiff that you're snooping around, he'll bury anything incriminating so deep, no amount of digging would ever uncover it.

No, in order to win the spy game, you've got to be cautious, methodical, and smart, like a master detective. And I can help with that. After all, I didn't earn my private investigator's badge by *not* knowing how to spy.

PRIVATE INVESTIGATOR

SEX   HAIR   EYES
M   **BLACK**   **GREEN**

This license certifies the holder's knowledge and expertise in the art of spying, tailing, snooping, and generally "getting to the bottom of things." If you've got secrets, he'll find them.

NAME: **MAX CORRIGAN**

OK, I may have actually just printed that myself on the school copy machine, but whatever—I've still got the skills to back it up. And I can show you everything I know.

So follow my advice to uncover Austin's innermost secrets.

HOW TO SPY ON SOMEONE LIKE YOU'RE A CIA AGENT

The target's been acquired.

Spying can be used to learn all kinds of private things, ranging from what presents your parents are giving you for your birthday to whether or not a guy or girl secretly likes you. Here's my guide for digging up someone's most classified information.

TAIL 'EM

You can learn tons about a person by following them for a day. Just create a disguise so you won't be noticed, stay a safe distance back, and record anything interesting you see. When people think they aren't being watched, that's when you'll discover who they really are.

STAKE OUT THEIR USUAL HANGOUT SPOTS

Instead of following people around, you can also hide out in places you know they'll be and let them come to you. Just make sure you go to the bathroom first or you could be in some serious trouble later!

DIG UP DIRT. LITERALLY.

OK, this is gonna sound gross, but people's garbage contains some of their best kept secrets. If you really want to learn what they're hiding, dig through their trash. Guaranteed, you'll discover things about them that you never thought you would!

USE INFORMANTS

Informants are a great asset to any spy. Find someone you can trust who hangs out with your target and bribe them to get information for you. They don't even have to be their friend—they just need to be harmless enough that your target feels free to talk around them without suspecting the information will ever leak back to you.

GO HI-TECH

Toys and gadgets are a necessity for any professional spy. However, if you don't have fancy equipment, you can get by with just your cell phone. Simply leave it on to record in a hidden location near where you know your target will be and then discreetly pick it up the moment they're gone. You'll have all kinds of secret info that you can play back again and again and again!

GO UNDERCOVER

Finally, if you're totally fearless, you can try infiltrating your target by buddying up to them in disguise. Be careful, though, because if your cover gets blown, your spying days will be over!

SPY GEAR

Never go out into the field empty-handed. These useful items are things that no self-respecting spy should be without:

 Cell phone. For taking photos, recording video, and keeping track of time.

 Small mirror. Useful for looking around corners.

 Notepad and pen. To record any useful information.

 Binoculars. Essential for long-distance viewing.

 Sunglasses. To shield your eyes and protect your identity.

 A variety of disguises and props. For slipping into and out of so you won't be discovered.

Man, I can't believe all that stuff you uncovered about Austin! Who knew? However, while it's all pretty eye-opening material, none of it is enough to bring down his campaign.

But at least we managed to follow him to his daily strategy session with Hailee. I just pray that it yields something we can use.

Holy smokes! That's it—the smoking gun! Whatever's in his permanent records holds the key to destroying Austin's political ambitions once and for all! Find it, and the presidency will finally be yours! #Success!

There's just one major problem: Austin's permanent records are stored in the vice principal's office. And she'll never let you access them. The only way you'll be able to get to them and win the presidency . . .

. . . is to break in.

CHAPTER TWENTY-SIX

The Crying Game

OK, don't freak out. I know this is major, but you can do this—you've already come so far. And this is the only thing standing in your way of winning the election. Get inside the vice principal's office and expose whatever's inside Austin's permanent records, and he'll be out of the running. You'll be giving your acceptance speech, and the school will have the leader it deserves!

Now, I'm not gonna lie—breaking into Vice Principal Hartley's inner sanctum won't be an easy undertaking. The place is more highly guarded than Fort Knox. There's always *somebody* watching it.

Not to mention, it's located within the main office, so that adds an extra layer of security. In fact, only the vice principal *herself* could fully give you access. And it's not like she's gonna just get up and leave you alone in there to rifle through all her things at a moment's notice.

Or maybe she will . . .

Remember how the vice principal said she might fetch you a cookie from the cafeteria if you ever came to her with a problem? Well, what if you came to her with a big problem? Like something so earth-shattering she'd get you a million cookies just to make you feel better! She'd totally leave you alone!

Get her to vamoose for a few minutes, and I'll sneak in once she's gone, search the joint with you, and bolt with

Austin's records before she comes back! It's a plan so dyna-mite, it's practically explosive!

Of course, for this strategy to be successful, Vice Principal Hartley can't have any doubts. You'll have to be so convincing even the biggest hater would crack open their heart at the sight of you. And the only way to do that is to cry like a baby.

Now, you may think crying on command is hard, but I have ways of faking it. I can train you to blubber uncon-trollably at the drop of a hat.

So follow these tips and I'll show you everything you need to turn on the waterworks.

HOW TO CRY ON COMMAND LIKE A HOLLYWOOD ACTOR

It's just so sad!

Being able to cry at the drop of a hat is a skill every kid should know. It can get you out of a jam in a heartbeat by creating major sympathy. To start the waterworks flow-ing, try these handy methods.

Drag up your most heart-wrenching memories.

R.I.P., Señor Mittens. You'll always be missed.

Chew on a hot pepper when no one's looking.

Ooh, those are some **spicy** tears!

Put a small amount of mentholated lip balm or Vicks VapoRub under your eyes.

As an added bonus, I can totally breathe better!

⚠ **WARNING:** BE **EXTRA CAREFUL** NOT TO GET ANY **IN** YOUR EYES—IT WOULD BE **BAD**!

Keep your eyes open as long as possible without blinking.

The tears will start flowing naturally!

Pinch yourself, bite your cheek, or pluck a nose hair.

It hurts **so much!**

Secretly squirt eyedrops in your eyes.

I just need a minute . . .

Fighting Back the Tears

Sometimes the best way to fake-cry is to not cry at all. Instead of going for the big act, reel it in and fight back the tears for a subtler performance. You won't have to act as hard and you'll earn sympathy points for your emotional bravery! That's an Oscar-worthy performance!

No . . . No . . . I promised myself I wouldn't cry. I'm good. I'm good.

Heh, heh, heh.

OK, here we are.

Now go in there and let the tears fly. And hold nothing back! Vice Principal Hartley better fall for this, 'cuz if you blow it, you—and everyone else in this school—really *will* have something to cry about.

CHAPTER TWENTY-SEVEN

Moved

Don't be embarrassed—crying happens to the best of us. Believe me, there are some days when I just go home, get into my sweatpants, and cry all night while watching *Animal Planet*. We've all been there.

Tell you what: Why don't you take a few moments to collect yourself? I'm going to run to the cafeteria to get you some cookies. I think that will cheer you up.

When I return, we'll chat some more. If we put our heads together, I'm sure we can figure out a way to make all your problems disappear.

CHAPTER TWENTY-EIGHT

Permanent Record

Now—quickly—help me rummage around Vice Principal Hartley's office before she returns! We don't have much time to find Austin's records!

Shoot! I can't find the records! What about you?

Ahhhh yeah. This is it! Whatever's in this file is so damaging it could bring Austin's entire campaign down to its knees! It's everything we've been working for all week! Your victory will finally be ensured!

Well, what are you waiting for—open it up! Let's see what's inside!

Gotcha!

Marchman, Austin

What? What is this? I don't understand. I—

Oh no.

Oh God no.

It's a trap! Austin and Hailee must have known we'd spy on their conversation and break into the vice principal's office! We fell right into their hands!

This is terrible! A theft scandal like this could end you! The students will never trust you to lead them once they see this! Austin and Hailee must have planned this setup right after we won the debate! I can't believe it!

Hold on—if Austin and Hailee weren't the masterminds behind this, then who was?

No.

Freaking.

Way.

CHAPTER TWENTY-NINE

Bloodless Coup

How naive. That was just a ruse to lull the students into a false sense of security. What I am is a snapping turtle. Slow. Steady. Unassuming. And then, when the moment's right, I snap. And I've been orchestrating this election the entire time to help Austin win.

See, Principal Sitz's tenure was up for review. And it was

time for me to become principal. So I created a plan to overthrow him. I knew that if I could show the school board just how much more effective I was, they'd promote me instead.

So I booked Sitz on an educational conference for the month to get him out of the way and then secretly set about remaking the school in my own image. And it's one of complete domination.

I'll start by removing the vending machines so students will be easier to control without their daily sugar rush. Then, I'll slash operating costs by getting rid of frivolous classes like art and dance. Finally, I'll create a strict dress code to stamp out all forms of individuality. By the time I'm finished, the word *fun* will be erased from the middle school vocabulary. There will be only discipline. Sweet, controlled discipline.

The only problem is, in order to enact these extreme changes before Principal Sitz returns, I need a class president to support my agenda without question. And that's where Austin comes in.

Austin's family and mine go way back—I've known him for years. And I've never met anyone so motivated to get ahead. Or with the financial means to do so. With a little inside help, I knew he'd easily win the election. So we struck a deal: I'd ensure his victory and he'd support all my policies once he was president. It was a marriage made in heaven.

Wait, Austin. I didn't know you were working with the vice principal.

Why would you agree to do such an awful thing?

Because once I'm class president, it'll be a cinch to get into an exclusive high school.

And then I can get into an Ivy League college.

And then the best law firm in the country.

And then Capitol Hill.

And then, finally, the White House.

Ultimate power.

But what about all the kids here?

I can help them much better when I'm running the country.

In thirty or so years.

See, Austin plans long-term. And so do I.

Unfortunately, the one thing we didn't plan on was you. I warned you not to enter the race, but you didn't listen. And once you started beating Austin, something had to be done.

So I set up this trap after the debate to discredit you.

And you fell right into it. And now that you've been busted stealing files, the whole school will know about your lack of moral character. You'll never win the election, and I'll finally have everything I want.

And it looks like your downfall's already begun. Austin's photo's been tweeted out to every kid with a cell phone. The students will be all over it in a matter of minutes, and your presidential run will go down in flames. A fitting end to such a fiery campaign.

Now, if you'll excuse me, I need to start taking some measurements for my new office. Because after tomorrow's election, Principal Sitz's job will soon be mine. And so will the school.

Consider yourself dismissed.

Oh, and did you still want that cookie?

CHAPTER THIRTY

Beaten

No way—I can't believe it! All this time, Austin and the vice principal have been working together! They've been colluding to bend the school to their own twisted agenda! And now they're going to destroy your campaign! We've got to split before the press skins you alive!

Oh man—it's worse than I thought!

Come on! We gotta get outta here! Quick! Before you're ground into dust!

Run!

Run!

This is not good. Like *seriously* not good. There's no amount of spin I could throw on this to make it disappear. Now that the school's got hold of this scandal, your presidential dreams are over. You'll be ruined!

I'm so sorry. I thought we could actually change things and make a difference, but we can't—the system's been rigged from the start, just like in all politics. And, because I didn't realize that, you, my dad, and every kid in this school are going to suffer. This is all my fault.

You should do yourself a favor and get as far away from me as possible, 'cuz I'll only bring you down further.

Seriously, go on and get outta here.

I'm not kidding. Go.

It's over. They won. We lost.

The end.

There's nothing left to do but give your concession speech. It's just too bad, 'cuz I *really* wanted you to win.

See, the thing is, even though I assist kids all the time, at the end of the day, I'm still just another one of 'em in a world controlled by adults. And I thought that by helping you become class president, it'd kinda be like *I* was class

CHAPTER THIRTY-ONE

Election Day

What are *you* doing here? Didn't I tell you to avoid me like

the plague? There's no way you can win this thing now.

And it's too late anyway. The vice principal and Austin's evil

plans are already under way. They just enacted their first

reform measure by removing the vending machines from

the cafeteria.

president, too. And, together, we could actually change the school.

But I guess that was just a silly, childish dream.

We should go to the gym and admit defeat before the final remarks start and the polls open. It's not like we could do anything to revive your campaign anyway. At least not alone.

What is she doing here? I thought she was on Team
Austin.

I'm here
to help.

CHAPTER THIRTY-TWO

S'more Help

The only reason I did was because I wanted to make a name for myself. By helping him achieve victory, everyone would be impressed with my skills. I could sit at the popular kids' table for once and hang out with the coolest cliques and go to the best parties. And I was prepared to do that at any cost.

But now that I know the full extent of his and the vice principal's plans, it's not worth it. Nothing is. Because, after this election is over, I'll still have to go to this school. And so will every other student here. And my conscience could never live with the fact that I helped turn this place into a virtual prison cell.

Austin can't be allowed to become class president, and there's only one candidate who can stand up to him.

You.

I've seen what you and Max have accomplished in just a week, and it's incredible. And, yes, Max and I may have had our differences in the past, but that's just politics. I'm still the same girl from summer camp who let him eat all my s'mores, and he's still the kid who stayed up all night to make sure raccoons didn't scratch through my tent. We can do this. Together.

I don't know exactly how, but I know this: I will help you in any way I can. If you want me to, that is. So, please, let me join your team to make sure you become the next class president of William H. Taft Middle School.

CHAPTER THIRTY-THREE

The Secrets to Becoming Class President

Wow. I would never have thought Hailee would be helping *us*. And, before you say anything, I didn't guard her tent 'cuz I liked her, OK? I guarded it 'cuz I didn't want her to get bitten and develop rabies and go and attack everyone at Camp Thunderbird. It was pure self-preservation.

Anyway, I just wish I knew what to do. Even if we're all in this together, I still don't have a clue how you'll be able to win this race.

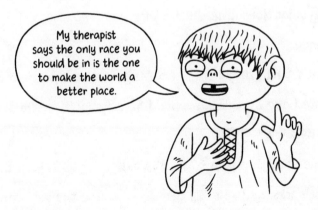

My therapist says the only race you should be in is the one to make the world a better place.

Holy smokes, that's it! All that mumbo jumbo Kevin's been spouting since day one is the answer! I know how you can still win the election and save the school: We implement the final part of my presidential strategy—*reputation*. We'll prove you're the candidate who will do anything to make this place better!

See, all this time you've been running for the wrong reasons. Being class president isn't about power or politics or gaming the system. It's about putting the school's needs before your own and making it the best place it can be. And it's time you started doing that.

If you can prove that, despite your scandal, you're the person who cares the most for this school and is willing to do whatever it takes to improve it, the kids will come around and vote for you! We just have to give the school what it needs.

And what does it need more than anything else?

Money.

That's why the lunch is inedible and the equipment is outdated and everything around here stinks. This school is broke as a joke!

Come up with a plan to fix the budget crisis before the final remarks, and kids will clearly see you're the best candidate for the job! And, luckily, you still have some influential supporters. By harnessing their skills, you can create a massive fund-raiser that will have everyone contributing to make this school great again! It could be your victory party!

Tell me that wouldn't be epic!

So come on, we better ask your peeps before it's too late!

Whoa, excellent idea! I can write a grant proposal that'll inspire organizations to give till it hurts!

I'll create a film that highlights all the problems this school has! People won't be able to resist helping out!

We'll throw a benefit concert that'll make fans open up their hearts **and** wallets!

I'll raffle off a month's worth of catered home-cooked meals! That should bring in some **primo dollars!**

Subject: Re: Help!
From: Chatter Chick
To: The New Kid
Date: Friday

I'll promote the fund-raiser on my blog! Every kid in the building will know about it!

—CC

And I'll ask the teachers and faculty to help out, too.

Excellent! But we're not done yet. We need all hands on deck to gather more participants. That means we've got to get Kevin Carl's head back in the game. He'll have some amazing ideas.

Come on, buddy. We need your brilliance. I know you're in there somewhere . . .

Positive energy is the path to happiness . . .

Positive energy is the path to happiness . . .

Darn it! He's not snapping out of it!

Unless . . .

197

Heh–heh. I think I might have gotten through.

Whoa. We may have just unleashed a monster. I only hope

Kevin helps us with our plan.

Well, that didn't go quite how I thought. But at least Kevin's finally doing *something*. And so should you.

While Hailee and I are out getting other people to sign up for the fund-raiser, you need to work the hallways to get every last vote you can. That means it's time to go full-on presidential. You need to make the school think that you're cut from the same cloth as the greats, like Washington and Lincoln—that you have the goods to run this school. In other words, you need to appear like a born leader.

Now, everything I've taught you has led up to this—it's my final lesson as your campaign manager. So pay attention, 'cuz this is . . .

HOW TO BE PRESIDENTIAL

Appearing presidential is more than just looking the part—you have to behave in ways that will make kids want to follow you to the ends of the earth and back. Here's how to come off like a commander in chief ready to rule the school.

REMEMBER EVERYONE YOU MEET

Class presidents meet tons of kids while campaigning for office—so many, in fact, that it can be hard to remember who everyone is! However, what sets a born leader apart from an average kid is that they're able to commit everyone's names and details to memory and call them up whenever they see them. So do that! You'll make voters feel important, and your approval rating will go through the roof! (And check out the sidebar on page 201 to learn my awesome name-remembering technique!)

Want to remember anyone's name? Try using
NAME ASSOCIATION

Simply make a hilarious association with someone's name the first time you meet them and then call it up again any time afterward to remember it. For instance, if a girl's name is Pam, think of a word that rhymes with it, like jam. Then picture Pam as a piece of toast, spreading jam all over herself. You'll never forget that! The next time you see her, all you have to remember is that jam rhymes with Pam and, presto—instant recall!

GREET EVERY KID WITH A KILLER HANDSHAKE

Shaking hands is a huge part of becoming class president. It shows respect, builds instant rapport, and tells voters everything they need to know about you. So greet all the kids you encounter with a handshake that's totally *on point*. You'll appear ready to take office!

THE
ULTIMATE
PRESIDENTIAL HANDSHAKE

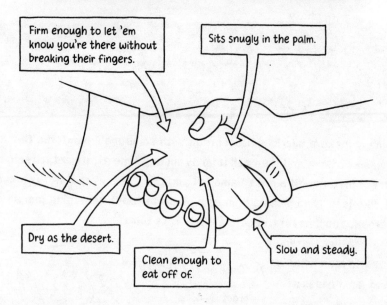

Firm enough to let 'em know you're there without breaking their fingers.

Sits snugly in the palm.

Dry as the desert.

Clean enough to eat off of.

Slow and steady.

HANDSHAKES TO AVOID

The Crusher

The Dead Fish

The Wet 'n' Wild

The Too Low

The Too High

The Violently Fast

The Stinker

The What in the—?

LISTEN TO YOUR CONSTITUENCY

A good president listens to every voter—even the crazy ones who should be committed to an insane asylum. So, when talking to the masses, use your ears more than your mouth. Ask questions. Take notes. Make eye contact so voters feel like you're giving them your full attention, even if your mind's totally wandering. Most of all, make the conversation more about *them* than *you*. By doing that, you'll win over ninety-nine percent of the people you meet!

But enough about me—let's talk more about your thoughts on the annual pizza party.

I was thinking, what if, instead of pizza, it was **raw meat**? And the entire party was **zombie-themed**!

Interesting . . .

Finally, someone who listens to my ideas!

KEEP IT CLASSY

Look, we all love a good fart or burp. However, as class president, you're held to a higher standard since everything you do reflects on the school. So act like a leader by projecting a presidential image of class, dignity, and sophistication.

DO

- Say "Please" and "Thank you."
- Blow your nose with a tissue.
- Hold the door.
- Cover your mouth when you cough or sneeze.
- Excuse yourself if you accidentally belch.
- Hold in any "bathroom-related urges."
- Use silverware when you eat.
- Dress nicely.

DON'T

- Talk like a drunken sailor out on shore leave.
- Pick your nose and flick the boogers clear across the hallway.
- Push people out of the way and trample over them to get to your class before anyone else.
- Hack a massive loogie so big it could fill a pool.
- Burp so loudly dogs can hear you in neighboring towns.
- Rip a juicy one and then laugh like a hyena.
- Put an entire meal in your mouth at one time and see if you can chew it.
- Kick off your shoes and socks in class and show everyone your dirty, stinky toes.

LEAD BY EXAMPLE

Lastly, kids want a leader that gives them hope, not drowns them in negativity. To act like a total baller commander in chief, treat people the way you would want to be treated. Find something nice to say about everyone—even your sworn enemies. Exercise fairness. And showcase your killer sense of humor to keep the mood light. By making voters feel good, they'll make you feel good, too—when the final ballots are cast!

All right, you're now everything a president should be. So go gather votes while Hailee and I enlist more people to help with the fund-raiser. I'll see you in the gym in an hour for the final remarks.

CHAPTER THIRTY-FOUR

Final Remarks

That was some great last-minute campaigning you did. I heard you swayed some crucial votes back in your favor. Now we just need to grab the rest of 'em.

And, for that, it all comes down to your fund-raiser. If

only Hailee would get here with the final confirmations! She better hurry—the vice principal's calling you up now!

Shoot, where is she? She was supposed to be here ten minutes ago! If this was all another part of Austin and Hailee's plan to trick you, I don't even know what I'll do! I'll never forgive this and—

Yes! She came through!

Everyone, before you vote, you should know the New Kid was able to come up with a plan to help fix the school's budget deficit.

If elected, the New Kid has pledged to make the presidential victory party the biggest fund-raising event this school's ever seen!

There will be musicians, and films, and food, and art, and performances! It'll raise insane money!

Not only that, but we'll close the financial gap further by reaching out to parents and neighbors and governors and senators, too! Year-round!

It'll be a community effort the likes this city's never seen!

Whoa! Governors and senators! That's ambitious! But that's why Hailee's one of the greats—she thinks big!

With the money we raise, we can turn this school around.

The book club will be able to thrive with fresh, current literature.

The library will be the hippest spot in school!

The film society can show movies in the epic ways they were meant to be seen.

You haven't lived until you've watched Batman on celluloid!

The musically gifted among us can let their voices sing out loud and clear.

This band room will finally have some working instruments!

Journalists exposing corruption of the highest order will be able to afford a platform.

Chatter Chick 😎 ≣

The press will stay free—the way it was intended to be!

The cafeteria food will get a healthier and tastier upgrade.

Say good-bye to Chicken Bake Surprise and hello to awesomeness!

The faculty can finally teach us with methods that are both entertaining **and** educational.

I could use the money to get new lab equipment! Ooh, the amazing experiments I could do!

And every student will have a bright, secure future.

Remember how I said I didn't like Hailee? Well, I admit, I may have been lying a little. She's amazing.

OK, I full-on like her all right! As in, *like* like her. I mean, how could you not! But I swear, you better not tell anyone. This is just between us.

Not between us, though, is this election. The whole school now sees how awesome you are—they're coming around to your side!

This is it—the moment we've all been waiting for! The tide is turning! And the final remarks are almost over! The students will start voting for you any minute! You're gonna win the election and be declared class president and defeat Austin and—

Oh no.

CHAPTER THIRTY-FIVE

Riches to Rags

I can buy the school *anything* to vote for me. Whatever it takes. I'll even have my dad fly out Beyoncé to personally hang out with every student for a day.

Face it, New Kid, you just can't compete. Now step aside so I can let everyone know what else I intend to purchase for them to secure my victory and—

Kevin Carl? What is that little mongrel doing here?

What? What is he talking about?

No way! That's not possible! Why would I believe anything an untrustworthy liar like Kevin Carl says?

What! No! It can't be! No!

This is not fair! It's not! It's—!

CHAPTER THIRTY-SIX

Hail to the Chief

Holy smokes! I can't believe it! Without Austin's bankroll, he's completely flailing! See, I told you he was all flash and no substance! And the students are finally realizing it, too!

And now that the students are seeing it, it's clear just how much better you are!

And not a moment too soon—the polls just opened and the voting's begun!

This is amazing! I don't even think we're gonna need to take a tally—this election is yours! You've won! You did it!

This is incredible! I just wish I knew how Kevin Carl was able to make all that happen. I've never seen anything so epic!

Man, that was devious! Thank goodness Kevin's on *our* side.

Now we just need to deal with the only other person left who isn't. Since you're president, may I suggest a first order of business? We take out the trash.

And there you have it! In only five short days, you've gone from average kid to class president. You went up against the greatest and watched them fall. You've seen the lows and now you're standing at the top. You are the rightful leader of this school.

There's only one issue left to make it official . . .

Where do you want to have your victory party?

SATURDAY

CHAPTER THIRTY-SEVEN

Victory Party

I'm not gonna lie—getting you elected was a little harder than I thought. But I *did* promise you were gonna win in a landslide victory. And I remained true to my word—you got a staggering majority of the votes.

Not only that, but thanks to this massive fund-raiser, you've raised almost $10,000 for the school so far! Everybody pulled together to help.

Plus, with all the outreach kids will be doing, we should be able to keep that number growing. The school will finally get the TLC it needs!

And it's all because of you. The school needed a leader and you stepped up. You made everybody's lives better. And since all the favors you owed will soon be fulfilled, you can start your term with a fresh slate. You're beholden to no one— no agenda, no allegiances, no backroom deals to adhere to. You're the fresh face of politics this school so sorely needed.

As for the old faces, they're on their way out. Austin's already put in for a school transfer, and Vice Principal Hartley has been suspended. Once I told my dad, he immediately rushed home and reported her to the school board.

And because he was so impressed by our performance, he said he'd even allow gum in the school! At least for a trial period anyway, which is a huge victory! Plus, he let us throw this party in the gym, and that's pretty sweet.

It's just too bad that Lewis is still stuck in the bathroom and can't join us. I keep telling him to go light on the dairy, but he doesn't listen. The good news, though, is he made a friend. Apparently Hailee has her own assistant

with an overactive bladder, and they've been chatting on
the phone for hours!

And speaking of Hailee, we couldn't have done it without her. Or Kevin Carl, for that matter. They were essential.
Which made me realize something.

Now that you're class president, you're gonna need a lot
more help than even I might be able to give you. You'll re-
quire people from all ends of the spectrum to assist you.

That's why I'm happy to say that Kevin and Hailee are
officially partnering with me. As of today, my company will
be stronger, smarter, and more efficient than it's ever been.

And you're totally gonna need our advice, 'cuz there are a lot of things to do as class president—the first of which is organizing the school dance. And that's gonna take some *real* work.

But don't worry about that right now—it can wait. For the moment, let's just get down and celebrate your victory. You earned it.

After you, Prez.

Acknowledgments

If I were elected president, my cabinet would be as follows:

Vice President
Erica Finkel

Department of Beautification
Chad W. Beckerman

Department of Communications
Caitlin Miller

Department of Corrections
Rob Sternitzky

Department of Printing
Kathy Lovisolo

Department of Traffic
Jim Armstrong

Chief of Staff
Charlie Kochman

Council of Advisors
Justin Rucker
Laura Geringer Bass

I could not have made this book without any of you. Thanks so much for all your help, your skills, your guidance, and your time to make this book what it is. You guys are the best, and I'm so lucky to have had your involvement.